I0778574

The Assorted Burdens of Parenthood

Alex De-Gruchy

The Assorted Burdens of Parenthood

Radical Bookshop and Press
4838 Richard Road SW, Suite 300
Calgary, AB T3E 6L1

FIC029000 - Fiction, Short Stories

July 1, 2025

Editor: Nadine Brito
Cover Design: Lexie Angelo

Typeset in Elza

ISBN-13: 978-1-990201-20-2

Printed in the United States

*For my mother and father,
for always giving me a home to come back
to, whenever and wherever I roam.*

contents

The Assorted Burdens of Parenthood

I woke up, which was unfortunate.

Disorientated, I opened bleary eyes. I was lying down. Everything hurt. I shifted slightly, which only made the pain worse, so I stopped moving and closed my eyes again. Apparently I'd gotten drunk and had the tar knocked out of me. I was familiar with the aftereffects of both.

"Morning." A man's unwelcome voice, grating. I ignored it but then there came the sound of tin banging against wood in quick succession. "I know you're awake. Get up. I wanna talk."

With some effort I sat up, swinging my legs over the side of the cot on which I'd been laying. I gasped as a sharp bolt of pain flared in my side and instinctively placed a hand there, as if that would do anything.

I was in a jail cell that took up a corner of the room. Metal bars built into the floor and ceiling, locked door on one side. The only things in my cell were a rusty cot with a thin straw mattress, a bucket, and a puddle of dried vomit on the floor.

"That was you who aired the paunch, in case you were wondering," said the man, nodding at the vomit. A lawman, judging by the metal star pinned to his waistcoat. He was sat behind the larger of the room's two desks, his a medium-sized rolltop, the other barely more than a simple school desk. He was slim, with swept-back brown hair, and looked to be in his twenties. In one hand he held a tin cup, on his face a troubled look.

"Water," I croaked, rubbing sleep from my eyes and a hand over my stubbled, aching jaw.

"Sure," the lawman said. "Soon as we've had a little talk."

He set down his cup, stood and walked around to the front of his desk, a gunbelt around his waist and a Colt resting in the holster on his right hip.

I noticed the sound of rain and looked towards one of the room's two windows to see water lazily streaming down the glass, the room's interior cold and gloomy, a small mercy: nothing worse than a hangover in the heat. The room seemed to make up the entire one-story building apart from a small closet beyond an open archway, two doors at the front and rear of the building leading outside. Pinned to a wall were several posters and notifications, while attached to the back wall was a locked gun rack. A lit stove occupied a corner, a coat stand and a lopsided, waist-height dresser nearby.

"You're lucky you're not dead," the lawman said.

"Lucky." I moved my tongue inside my mouth and winced as it prodded a loose tooth. "That's me."

"Well, the alternative was you getting beat to death by Dewey and his friends. They gave you a real lacing and wouldn't've let up if Ira hadn't taken out his sawn-off from behind the bar."

One of my nostrils was clogged so I lowered my head, pressed a finger against the opposite nostril and blew. A wad of congealed blood flew out of my nose and hit the floor.

The lawman frowned. "My name's David Boyd. I'm the Marshal of Lorelai. That's the town you're in, by the way."

It was news to me. I could barely remember anything of the past few days. It had been a long time since I'd been on a bender like that.

"What's your name?" Boyd asked.

"Corwin."

"First name?"

"Joe." I'd used it before, a name as good as any.

"You remember much of last night, Joe?"

I shook my head. Gently.

Marshal Boyd began to tell me how I'd been seen riding into Lorelai the previous evening, already drunk, before heading straight for Ira's, the towns' one saloon, leaving my horse, Eliza, untied outside. I attached myself to the bar and proceeded to drink whiskey. A *lot* of whiskey. At some point Dewey, Jim and Sylvester, three men who worked as hands for a local rancher named George McMahon entered and took a place next to me at the bar. According to Ira, words were exchanged between the ranch-hands and I, this brief conversation ending with me telling Dewey to go fuck himself. The ranch-hands took umbrage to this and came at me swinging. I got in a couple of licks—Jim ended up with a broken nose and Dewey's balls had an encounter with my boot—but soon went down and the men beat me until Ira's shotgun came into play. Boyd was summoned, and my battered, unconscious body was hauled to the Marshal's office.

"I sent Dewey and the others back to McMahon's to cool off," Boyd said, "but they're not gonna forget you anytime soon."

"They wanna try to finish the job, I'm right here."

"I've got no intention of letting you die while you're in my custody. Besides, like I said: I wanna talk."

Boyd went to the closet and retrieved my satchel and saddlebags. He placed them on his desk and began to open them. "Your Winchester and hat are in there too, I've got your pistols and knife in my desk. Your horse and rig are in Luke Nichols' livery."

Boyd rifled through my satchel and saddlebags, listing off some of the contents: a bill of sale and some grain for Eliza, my matches and makings, a gun-cleaning kit, ammunition, a whetstone, spare clothes, a water canteen.

"At first I figured you for just a no-account barrel-boarder, Joe." Boyd took out a small glass jar containing a black and pale-red eyeball floating in brine. "But then I wasn't so sure."

He held up the vial, looking at the inhuman eye, a small tail of optic nerve still attached, then flinched as the eyeball swivelled in his direction.

Boyd set down the vial and continued taking out more items: a bone bearing a host of carved symbols and which served as a talisman of protection against certain curses; an iron crucifix, the ends of which I'd filed down to sharp points; a pouch of ashes which never lost their heat, for use in certain spells; and a tattered journal which had belonged to the vampire-hunting order named the Brothers of the Dawn.

Boyd stopped there.

"My daddy always taught me to keep an open mind. And I've seen some things in my time, unnatural things I can't explain, so I try not to be quick to dismiss something as balderdash. So, I wanna know who you are. Because you might be able to help me."

I told Boyd his initial impression was right: I *was* just a deadbeat. I just happened to be one who long ago learnt that the world which most people spent their entire lives thinking they existed in was just the surface, that beneath that lay another world of darkness and strangeness, an unforgiving world of ghosts and the undead, demons and monsters, sorcery and secrets. It was a world I never wanted anything to do with but could never seem to avoid for long, hence why I carried the things I did, to help me stay alive. I didn't tell Boyd I couldn't remember the last time I had an actual reason to want to do that.

"Look at me, Marshal," I concluded, the smell of vomit in my nostrils, my mouth sour, head pounding. "Do I look like someone who's of any use to anyone?"

Boyd looked out of a window. "I have a daughter. Sophia. Eight years old. There's something wrong with her. Has been for a few weeks. Our local doctor visited her a couple of times but couldn't do anything. I guess I shouldn't be too surprised, because whatever's wrong with my little girl, it isn't... it isn't normal."

"I'm no doctor."

"No, but you know about these things. I want you to take a look at my daughter, see if you can tell me what's wrong with her, and how to fix it. You do, I'll let you go free. You don't, I'll see you charged with assault, disturbing the peace, maybe a few other things, and you can cool your heels in there until you stand before a judge."

I smiled bitterly then lay down on the cot and closed my eyes.

"Well?" Boyd asked.

"Happy to help," I said.

I sat on the edge of the cot, taking another sip of bitter coffee. Marshal Boyd had given me the drink along with a stale bread roll and a few pieces of beef jerky before he left to fetch his deputy. He wanted me sober. I couldn't imagine anything I wanted less, but still I drank the coffee and ate the food.

"You're a mess," a woman said from across the room.

I looked over and saw Claudia standing next to a window, arms folded, face turned to the glass as she stared at the rain. She wore the same dress she always did, her brown hair loose and flowing as usual. Though only one side of her face was visible, I could see she seemed sad.

I looked down at the dark patch of wooden floor where my pool of vomit had been, and from outside heard the rumble and clatter of a stagecoach as it passed by.

"I haven't seen you like this in a long time," Claudia said. "What's going on?"

"I'm tired."

"And you wanna rest by drinking yourself to death?"

"I've had worse ideas." *And at least this one won't get anyone killed besides me*, I thought.

"You don't wanna die."

I looked up at Claudia, who stared back at me. In the dismal morning her brown eyes were even darker than usual, contrasting with her pale skin. "So what *do* I want?" I asked, my tone as bitter as my coffee.

"Something you can't have," she said softly. "So you need to think of something else. Before you throw away what life you've got left."

I let out a derisive breath. "What a waste *that* would be."

I squeezed my eyes shut and pinched the bridge of my nose. *My fucking head...*

I heard the front door open and I opened my eyes to see Marshal Boyd enter with a younger man following behind, rainwater dripping from their hats and coats. As the younger man shut the door, I saw the deputy badge on his chest.

"Alright, Pete, I'll be back when I can," Boyd said as he took a ring of keys from a coat pocket. "Don't come fetch me unless you absolutely have to, understand?"

As Boyd walked to my cell, Pete looked at me with scepticism. "You sure about this, Marshal? Might be he's more trouble sober than he was drunk."

Boyd inserted a key in the lock of my cell door. "He won't be any trouble. We have an understanding."

Before we left the jail, Boyd returned my hat and satchel but kept my saddlebags, knife and guns. We stepped out onto the rutted main street and I got my first sober look at Lorelai, just another dying, one-horse burg of grim- and tired-looking people, the place made all the more bleak by the rain.

The town was quiet, a few trudging horses here and there, a lone wagon rolling through thoroughfares of churned-up mud, men and women huddled into themselves from the chill as they hurried by, forced to navigate the mud via ragged wooden planks that had been laid down. The windows of the local businesses were dusty, their interiors cloaked in shadow, ornamented false fronts decaying. One building was a half-constructed timber shell, all efforts towards its completion seemingly having been abandoned long ago.

Maybe Lorelai had been poised to reap the benefits of a new railroad line only for it to pass the town by, or a local mine had been Lorelai's lifeblood until it ran dry. Boyd didn't volunteer any details and I didn't ask. I'd seen it all before: eventually the town would die, its people scattered to the winds.

Boyd had no intention of introducing me to his wife and daughter reeking of sweat, whiskey and vomit, so our first stop was the town's single, shabby hotel, where I was forced to pay for a bath. The water was cold, and the look the sour-faced owner gave me even colder. I was in the battered metal tub for barely five minutes before Boyd ordered me out. There was no time to do anything about my clothes, but I was somewhat more presentable.

Boyd's house was at the edge of town. As we walked there, he told me how Sophia had been sick at times in the past but no more than any normal child, but a few weeks ago she started exhibiting worrying behaviour: periods where she spoke in an unknown language, as though hypnotised. Brief seizures. She'd scribble meaningless lines and patterns on the floors and walls, and suffer anguished, violent outbursts. I didn't want to hear all this but clearly Boyd wanted to tell it even less.

Boyd's house was nicer and better maintained than most of the other properties I'd seen in Lorelai so far, with crisp green paint coating its two-storey exterior. I wiped what mud I could off my boots on the porch before I followed Boyd through the front door into a hallway which split the house down the middle, leading straight to a back door. The hallway had three closed doors leading off it, a couple of pieces of furniture, and a staircase leading up to the second floor.

As Boyd and I hung up our hats and coats on a hatstand, a woman emerged from an adjoining room, wearing a blouse and a bleached cotton skirt. She was blonde, thin and looked a little younger than Boyd, although you could be mistaken for thinking otherwise given the weariness and tension evident in her face and body language.

"Joe, this is my wife, Mary," Boyd said. "Mary, this is the gentleman I told you about."

I nodded to her. "Ma'am."

"Good morning," Mary said with a pinched expression.

"Is Sophia in her room?" Boyd asked. Mary nodded. He gave her arm a gentle squeeze. "Alright. We're gonna go talk to her."

I followed Boyd upstairs and we made our way to an open door.

Sophia's room would have been comfortable and pleasant were it not for the harsh, alien shapes and symbols scrawled all over the floor and walls, the pieces of furniture standing at odd angles or tipped over, and the floor being strewn with clothing and bedsheets.

Boyd looked around at the mess. "Sweetheart, your mother only cleaned up in here this morning…"

Sophia sat at the head of her bed atop a pillow. She held herself tightly, knees tucked up with her arms wrapped around her shins, feet bare, her dark hair hanging loose and messy, framing what little I could see of her face. Her blue eyes stared ahead, paying no attention to me or her father.

"Sophia, I've got a friend who wants to meet you," Boyd said. "He's going to help you feel better."

I felt a stab of hatred towards Boyd for saying such a foolish thing as I stepped towards the bed. Sophia winced as I neared, as if my approach were painful. I stopped.

"Stranger," Sophia said in a small voice. "Ghost. Walks in the dark."

The girl had me there: if there was ever a time I walked in the light, it was long ago. Wanting to get this over with, I said, "Hello, Sophia. My name's Joe."

"Your daughter has a condition," I told Boyd and Mary. "Very rare, but it happens. Most people go their entire lives unaware of the supernatural, or at most it's an unexplained chill down the spine, an instinctual feeling that something bad's in the air. But then the feeling passes and they go on with their lives. Then there are people like Sophia, born with a powerful sensitivity to the supernatural. They can't help but feel it, even if they don't understand it. It can affect a person in different ways, some worse than others. That's what you're seeing in Sophia's behaviour."

Boyd and Mary looked at me across the kitchen table, troubled. We sat in lanternlight, darkness falling early, the chill kept at bay by a lit stove as rain rattled against the house.

Mary shook her head, rubbing at one eye. "This is..." She trailed off into silence.

Boyd took his wife's hand. "Why now? She was fine before."

"My guess is simple proximity," I said. "Sophia's probably never been around anything supernatural in the past so there was nothing for her to react to. But now something's come close enough that it's affecting her. And it's still around. If it goes away, so should her symptoms. For now. You should realise, this is something she'll have to live with for the rest of her life."

Mary fixed her eyes on me, iron behind the glistening wetness now. "What's hurting my daughter?"

I took a swallow of the applejack Boyd had poured, the liquor strong and sweet and far better than coffee. Boyd took a smaller sip from his own glass. We were alone, Mary having retired for the night, Sophia in her own room, calm for now.

We sat on a bench seat on Boyd's back porch, the rear of his property a fenced-off patch of land containing a chicken coop, a small corn crib and a few vegetable patches. The rain had stopped and the night air was cool. The moon and stars were still obscured by clouds, though, and blackness loomed close beyond the pool of flickering lanternlight in which we sat, a set of steps leading down from the covered porch to the soaking grass beyond.

"I had a son," Boyd said. "William. Scarlet fever took him when he was just five years old. Mary and I, we... we can't lose Sophia too. What do we do?"

"Like I said, I have no idea what's causing this," I said. "Could be one of a million things. Whatever it is might move on and it'll vanish overnight."

"That's not good enough." There was a hard look on Boyd's face. "We have a deal. If you're no –"

"I didn't forget, Marshal." I wanted to close my eyes. Be anywhere but here. Hear no more about suffering. "Think back to when it started. Do you remember anything odd happening in town or hereabouts?"

"Not that I recall. Most common news these days is people leaving town, moving on to somewhere new. The week Sophia took a turn… I hauled Cutter Nelson in for breaking a couple of windows at the general store, the Bixbys came to me about their missing dogs, Clyde Farris threatened to kill his brother, but those two –"

"The Bixbys' dogs. Tell me about that."

"Not much to tell. Bixbys are a local family, had four dogs 'til three disappeared over the course of a week. No sign of anything odd, so I figured they just ran off."

"What about the doctor who visited Sophia?"

During my conversation with the girl, I'd done most of the talking. Most of what she said was disjointed and nonsensical, but there was something which stuck with me: she mentioned being visited by "a man of blood and whispers," which I thought might refer to the doctor.

"Amos Greenwood. He's been the doctor here since before we arrived, going on about eleven years. Family man, wife and two boys, Ned and Elton. The youngest, Elton, has a bum leg, can't get around without a stick, poor kid. Anyway, the doc's the quiet type but seems to know his job." Boyd hesitated.

"What?" I prompted.

"Amos hasn't been around much these past few weeks. Or as attentive in his duties, I guess, not like he usually is. He's been going hunting, so I'm told. I've never known him to. He's not exactly a born woodsman. There's been other talk too, I suppose."

"What talk?"

"Mary heard that Geraldine, Amos' wife, has been a bundle of nerves, something to do with Amos and life at home. Which is odd, since it's no secret Geraldine wears the pants in that marriage. But that's their business. With any luck they'll be right as rain when they come back."

"Come back from where?"

"A cabin they own outside town. Amos' father built it years ago, before he passed on and it ended up in the doc's hands. A few days ago the whole family took their wagon up there, no one knows when they're coming back. The boys have been missing their schooling. As for the doc, I appreciate a man's entitled to a break from his work, but without him around the closest thing Lorelai has to a doctor is the veterinarian. Why're you so curious about him anyway?"

I rubbed the back of my neck and downed the remainder of my liquor as a cold gust of wind whistled across the porch. "Maybe it's nothing, but I'd like to talk to Greenwood."

Boyd rose to his feet. "Then let's go."

"Marshal, I'm numb where I don't hurt and can hardly keep my eyes open. I need some rest if I'm gonna be of any use to you or your daughter. A few more hours won't make any difference." I didn't know that for a fact but my body couldn't go much longer without some sleep.

Boyd was silent for a moment. "Fine. But we head out before dawn."

Amongst shelves of cans and jars, I lay on the bedroll inside the small pantry on the ground floor of the Boyds' home and closed my eyes. The wooden floor beneath me was hard but my body was still grateful for it.

Claudia's voice came to me in the darkness. "I hope you can save the girl."

"Just doing what I can to get outta here," I muttered.

"We both know you could cut and run now if you really wanted."

"Let me sleep. You're not real."

"So you say. But even with all the peculiar people you've met who could prove it one way or the other, you've never asked one a' them to. Odd, ain't it? Maybe you're scared because you know you won't like the answer either way."

"If you're really a ghost then you're likely hurting the girl just by being here. Is that what you want?"

It was a lousy thing to say, but it had been a lousy day. If I got an answer then I didn't hear it as I sank into blackness.

It was still dark when Boyd woke me. The house was silent, Mary and Sophia upstairs, and within a few minutes the Marshal and I were out the door. We moved through town, a fine drizzle falling. The walk eased some of the stiffness in my body, my hangover gone, although I was still far from hearty as a buck. A few isolated figures moved through the streets, lanternlight flickering in a few buildings.

Boyd and I didn't speak until we arrived at Amos Greenwood's house and the small plot of land on which it stood. The building seemed vacant.

"Wagon's not here," Boyd said. "I guess they're still at the cabin."

We entered the yard and walked to the porch. Boyd knocked on the front door. A moment passed. "Doc? Mrs. Greenwood? It's Marshal Boyd." Still nothing. He turned to me. "There's a back door –"

I drove the sole of my boot into the front door, the noise loud in the stillness. The frame splintered and the door slammed against an interior wall.

Boyd's mouth hung open. "What the blazes are you doing?"

"Trying to wind up this business. Just like you want."

We went inside.

Boyd called out again, but received no response.

A lantern stood on a table near the front door and Boyd picked it up. He lit it then held it before him in his left hand, resting his right hand on his holstered revolver. I was very aware of the empty space on my belt where my own pistol should've been.

We searched the house but found nothing out of the ordinary, and no sign of the Greenwoods. The last place we checked was the cellar door, the only interior door with a lock – three sturdy padlocks, to be precise, all seemingly new.

"That's odd," Boyd said.

"Suspicious." I breathed in through my nose, picking up a faint odour of decay. "You smell that?"

Boyd sniffed.

"Yeah."

"Something's not right here."

Boyd went to the kitchen and returned holding a tarnished poker. He handed it to me. "Let's have a look-see."

It took over a dozen hits with the poker to break the three locks but eventually they lay on the floor and I pushed open the door. The smell of rot grew stronger. Wooden steps led down to the dirt floor of the cellar below, only a little of which could be seen in the flickering light that spilled from the lantern in Boyd's hand. Everything else was black.

I turned to Boyd.

"After you, Marshal."

Boyd glanced at me and the poker, seemingly taking a moment to decide if he could trust me not to brain him from behind. Then he took out his Colt and began to descend the stairs, the treads creaking beneath our boots until we reached the bottom. We stood there in the small space, the ceiling beams a few inches above our heads. Boyd held out the lantern and the light illuminated the whole room. Small bones and skulls were strewn across the floor, all animal in nature, a mixture of dogs, cats, squirrels and birds from what I saw, all stripped bare of any meat.

"Reckon we've found the Bixbys' missing dogs," I said.

Along with some sacks of flour and grain, various tools and loose pieces of timber, I noticed a few traps and other pieces of hunting equipment, which helped to explain the bones.

A table stood against the far wall. Boyd squinted towards an object that was on it. "What *is* that?"

I recognised what Boyd was looking at. I yanked the revolver out of his hand and strode towards the table, the gun outstretched before me, small bones crunching beneath my feet. The lanternlight swayed and flashed drunkenly around the room as Boyd moved behind me, calling after me, but my focus remained on the dark shape on the table until I stood before it, the revolver's muzzle inches from it.

Boyd hurried to my side. "What do you –"

"It's alright." I held Boyd's revolver out to him grip-first. "It's dead."

Boyd's eyes widened as he looked at the thing on the table. "Good God…"

Most of the table's surface was covered in a thick pile of straw, resting on which was the corpse. The limbless, slug-like creature was about the size of a fox, its slick, rubbery skin a mottled mixture of black and purple, the head exhibiting no features other than a fang-filled, circular mouth ringed by a number of short feelers. It had a deep gash running down one side of its body, a wound which at some point had been expertly stitched up - by a doctor's hand, I guessed. The thing had been dead at least a few days, the stench of decay thick.

At the back end of the corpse was an orifice which had ruptured, forming a puddle of congealed, black blood and innards. Lying amidst this was an infant, the creature no bigger than a small bird and as dead as the parent which had birthed it.

And it wasn't just black blood present – although it had dried and darkened, red blood covered much of the straw and the table beneath.

"It's a whisperer," I said. "That's the most common name I've heard, anyway. They live in dark and wet places: caves, underground rivers and such. And they have the power to influence people's minds."

"What? How - you mean this thing can control people?"

"Close enough. It can put ideas in your head. Ones which might seem crazy at first but then quickly become something you absolutely have to do."

"This... so is *this* what's been hurting Sophia?"

"I don't know. If so then your daughter should've recovered by now, it's been dead for days. Let's talk upstairs. It stinks down here."

Boyd and I stood in the Greenwoods' kitchen as I explained how I saw things. "At least one of the Greenwoods - most likely Amos - came into contact with that adult whisperer downstairs, likely somewhere outside town. It was pregnant, and Amos' mind was vulnerable to it. Judging by the creature's wound, I'd guess it influenced him to bring it home with him and try to heal it, to save it and the babies it was carrying, hence him sewing it up and hunting animals to feed it. I doubt his family knew about it if he hid it in the cellar and started locking the door, and whisperers usually can't influence more than one or two people at a time, and this one was hurt besides. This would explain Amos' odd behaviour. And I'd say this all started a few weeks back, when your daughter got sick."

"But the thing's dead now, so why isn't she better?" Boyd asked.

"That smaller whisperer was an infant, the mother had given birth. It was probably the strain of that that killed it. Whisperers

24

don't produce just one baby at a time, more like anywhere
between eight and fifteen. And since we didn't find them down
there, my guess is those other infants survived."

"You're saying they're what's still affecting Sophia?"

"Maybe. Either way, the Greenwoods are in danger."

The rain began to let up as Boyd and I rode out of town. I was
back in the saddle, Eliza beneath me, Boyd having returned my
horse along with the rest of my confiscated plunder, the Marshal
and I now headed for Amos' cabin.

We'd burnt the corpses of the whisperer and its child, and
I shared my suspicion that when the Greenwoods left for the
cabin, it was likely after the death of the adult and that the family
took the surviving infants with them, Amos probably having
fallen under their collective influence right after they were born,
alongside the death of their mother. One infant whisperer wasn't
as powerful as an adult, but enough of them together might be.

Boyd and I followed a trail which rose gradually into timbered
hills, the ground and woods still damp, our horses' breath
steaming in the air as we rode at a swift pace. We soon turned
off the main trail and onto a rougher, less defined path that
wound through trees, crowding brush and a shallow gully.

"Up ahead," Boyd said.

The one-storey cabin and the small clearing it occupied came
into view. The Greenwoods' wagon was parked out front, their
horse tied to a hitching post.

"We should play it quietly," I said. "You approach from the
front, I'll take the rear."

"Is that really necessary?"

"The doctor isn't himself, Marshal. Best not take chances."

We moved into a thicket of pines not far from a rear corner
of the cabin, hitching our horses to a couple of trees. The cabin
seemed solidly built, with good-quality logs securely notched,

though there were signs of neglect such as a few loose roof shingles. I'd seen a window and door built into the front wall and now saw the same in the rear wall as Boyd and I crept towards the edge of the thicket, each of us gripping a revolver.

Emerging from the treeline, the Marshal headed for the front corner of the cabin while I moved towards the rear corner. When I reached my spot I looked in Boyd's direction to see him disappear around the corner of the structure. I listened, hearing nothing but the typical noises of the woods, until a muffled thud sounded from inside the cabin. A few seconds later it repeated, continuing at similar intervals.

I kept close to the rear wall as I moved along it, ducking beneath the curtained window. My gaze moved to a nearby well, sitting atop the lip of which was Claudia. Her eyes were fixed on mine and there was a sad, knowing look on her face.

I continued on, reaching the rear door. Standing off to the side of it, I used my free hand to gently lift the latch. A powerful, coppery smell hit me and from the front of the cabin I heard a horrified Boyd exclaim, "Amos, what in God's name –"

I shoved the door open and stepped into the doorway to be greeted with a sight which I knew right then would stay with me the rest of my days.

The cabin interior consisted of a main room with a smaller, partitioned bedroom taking up one corner. There were also two cots off to one side, the wool blankets that covered their mattresses soaked through with blood from the corpses lying atop them: Elton and Ned Greenwood, both shot to death. A walking stick lay nearby.

On a table near the centre of the room lay Geraldine Greenwood, I presumed: I hadn't met the woman so wouldn't have recognised her even if the mutilated body still had its head, but that had been removed, along with both arms and a leg, the appendages crudely hacked off. Blood had pooled on the floor around the table.

Standing at a counter nearby was Amos Greenwood. Dishevelled and blood-soaked, he gripped a cleaver in his right hand, holding it in the air as his wild eyes shifted from Boyd to me. I realised the severed arm which Amos had been in the process of chopping up accounted for the rhythmic thudding I'd heard from outside.

On the floor near Amos was a wooden chest, its lid open, the interior largely filled with dirt, writhing in a tangled heap upon which were around a dozen infant whisperers. Visible among the mass of small, slick bodies was a chunk of human flesh that the creatures fed on.

I spotted the rifle leaning against the counter as Amos quickly turned towards Boyd and hurled the cleaver in the marshal's direction before picking up the gun and swinging it around towards me. I fired twice, my first bullet missing but my second hitting Amos in the ribs, although he barely stumbled as he fired back at me. I dodged, dashing outside the cabin.

"*Amos!*" Boyd cried before the rifle barked again.

Raising my Colt, I leaned around the doorframe and saw Amos charging through the open front door into Boyd. The two men tumbled out of sight, a shot sounding from the Marshal's revolver.

I ran through the cabin, being careful not to slip in blood. From the front yard I heard Boyd give an agonised scream.

I stepped through the doorway and found Boyd lying on his back, his right hand clamped around his left as he screamed, blood pouring between his fingers. Amos straddled him, the cleaver back in his hand, his rifle discarded. His head spun in my direction and he leapt to his feet and launched himself at me with a roar.

Taking a step back, I managed to fire once. Amos uttered a gurgle as the bullet tore through his neck, but then he was on me, cleaver swinging. Tangled together, we tumbled to the ground, my hat falling from my head, blood gushing from the hole in Amos' neck, his hissing and grunting loud in my ears as we sprawled in the mud.

I pinned Amos' cleaver arm beneath my body while he clawed at my face and neck with his free hand. Moving my Colt, I tried to jam the muzzle against his torso, but he ruined my aim as he twisted, and I fired only for the bullet to thud into the ground. Amos was losing a lot of blood but none of his strength or murderous rage, his body propelled by the influence of the infant whisperers.

I brought the grip of my Colt down on Amos' forehead once, twice, and the third blow stunned him enough to allow me to jam the muzzle up under his jaw. I pulled the trigger twice in quick succession, Amos' body jerking as both bullets emerged from the top of his skull, spraying blood, bone and brain. With a final grunt he went limp, and I rolled his body away, panting as I rose to one knee.

Amos lay unmoving, eyes blank as they stared up at the sky. Gouts of blood gently spurted from his shattered skull and ragged neck, his exposed, ruined brains no longer under the influence of a damn thing.

"How's the hand?" I asked Boyd.

"Still a few fingers lighter than it was."

It was the following morning and we were in Boyd's bedroom. I stood next to him as he sat propped up in bed, a sheet pulled up around his waist. His left hand was swaddled in bandages, Amos' cleaver having sliced off three of his fingers. I'd managed to keep the blood loss to a minimum at the cabin with a towel I found inside.

"The veterinarian did a decent job patching you up," I said.

"Wasn't like there was a doctor to do it." Boyd frowned. "What Amos did… that a man could do that to his own family…"

"The Amos we found at that cabin wasn't really the man you knew anymore, for what it's worth."

Boyd and I had already talked about how I figured the infant whisperers weren't satisfied with small animals so forced Amos to provide them with something more substantial. No doubt his family had no idea what he was planning when he took them out of town, or about the monsters hidden in their luggage. If we hadn't shown up, Amos would've fed the whisperers until the meat ran out, then gone looking for more.

I'd burnt the infant whisperers inside the stove at Amos' cabin, moving quickly as I fought the invasive tugging I felt inside my head as they tried to pull my strings like they had the doctor's.

Boyd had ordered his deputy to round up some men and bring the bodies of the Greenwoods back to town so they could be buried. The marshal's official story was that Amos had gone mad and murdered his family, Boyd wisely leaving out any mention of the whisperers. There was no evidence left of their existence, and he knew as well as I did that the townsfolk would think he'd lost his own mind if he told the whole truth.

Boyd looked up at me. "So now you'll be on your way."

"I'm fixing to."

"I know I bulldozed you with this whole thing, but thank you, Joe. For helping my daughter. My wife's equally grateful."

"Sure."

Sophia had already begun to show signs of recovery. Apparently she'd slept more restfully last night than she had in weeks, not to mention ate three portions of breakfast this morning. As for me, I'd spent another night on the pantry floor then made a point of smoking alone out on the porch while Mary fed her daughter. Yeah, the woman was grateful, but she didn't want me in her home and I didn't blame her.

Boyd looked at his bandaged hand. "Guess I'm in a fix. Not much use for a one-handed Marshal."

"Might be a good time to move on. Plenty of other places better than this."

"Maybe. But there's a lot to see about: the house, Sophia's schooling… I don't know."

The way the Marshal spoke didn't inspire confidence, but that wasn't my problem. If he wanted to stay in Lorelai and rot with it then that was his choice. I said my goodbyes, left the bedroom and descended the stairs, making no effort to say goodbye to Mary, who I could hear moving around in the kitchen.

Outside I walked to the hitching post where Eliza waited. I heard a tapping on glass from the house behind me, turned and saw Sophia standing at her bedroom window, looking down at me. Even with the distance and glass between us, I could see the troubled look on her face as she raised her hand in a wave. I touched the brim of my hat. Turning back to Eliza, I took hold of her reins.

As I untied the leather straps, Claudia appeared, looking up at Sophia. "Think she'll be okay?"

I glanced at Claudia, her hair blowing around her face. There was a bitter chill in the morning air, but the cold never bothered her.

"It's gonna be tough," I said. "It's a strange, dangerous world that never gets any less so, and she's more vulnerable to it than most."

"You ever think about being a father?"

"No."

"Did you ever think about it when we were together? We never talked about it."

"No."

30

It was a lie. Sure, I'd thought about fatherhood when Claudia was around, maybe a couple of times in the years since. But I'd never felt anything for another woman like what I felt for her. Besides, although I didn't like to admit it, I knew the truth: after what losing Claudia had done to me, I didn't think I was strong enough to risk losing someone else I loved. Things were better this way.

I mounted Eliza and turned her into the road, thinking of the reality of the lonely miles ahead and the two bottles of whiskey in my saddlebags, of whatever decay and blood and pain awaited, while burying pointless fantasies of things that would never be.

ABOUT THE AUTHOR

Alex De-Gruchy is a writer, editor and narrative designer whose work has included comic books, video games, prose, film, poetry, radio and other audio, and more. You can find a list of his credits to date at www.alexdegruchy.wordpress.com.